The Cleaning Witch

Close the school? Just when Grizelda had found herself the right job? No – not if *she* had anything to do with it!

Grizelda Grimthorpe fixed her bright green eyes on Miss Addle, twiddled her fingers – two bright purple sparks flew into the air – and muttered,

"Dirt and dust must now obey;
Grizelda Grimthorpe's come to stay!"

CECILIA LENAGH

The
Cleaning Witch

Illustrated by Serena Feneziani

To my parents –
a small return for their gift
of a childhood full of books.
C.L.

Scholastic Children's Books,
Commonwealth House, 1-19 New Oxford Street,
London WC1A 1NU, UK
a division of Scholastic Ltd
London ~ New York ~ Toronto ~ Sydney ~ Auckland

Published in the UK by Scholastic Ltd, 1997

Text copyright © Cecilia Lenagh, 1997
Illustrations copyright © Serena Feneziani, 1997

ISBN 0 590 13923 1

Typeset by Backup... Creative Services, Dorset
Printed by Cox & Wyman Ltd, Reading, Berks.

10 9 8 7 6 5 4 3 2 1

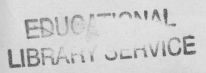

Chapter 1

Grizelda Grimthorpe was grumpy. Business just wasn't what it used to be.

"Nobody wants a witch these days," she muttered, rubbing furiously at her crystal ball with a duster. "I wish I had another job, indeed I do!"

As she spoke, the crystal ball glowed. Within it appeared the "Situations

Vacant" column from the *Grindley Echo*. Picked out in red was the small advertisement,

"Cleaner wanted. Apply Miss Addle's Academy for Artistic Children."

"Hmm! Speak when you're spoken to!" said Grizelda, throwing her duster over the crystal ball.

She stomped outside, looked for a moment at her sign –

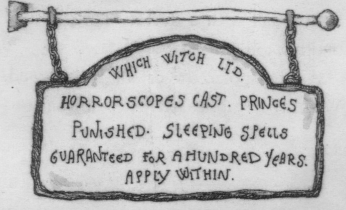

WHICH WITCH LTD.
HORRORSCOPES CAST. PRINCES
PUNISHED. SLEEPING SPELLS
GUARANTEED FOR A HUNDRED YEARS.
APPLY WITHIN.

– and sighed. "Must *be* about a hundred years since I frogged anyone," she said. "But, though I say so myself, when I frogged 'em, they *stayed* frogged!"

Ten minutes later Grizelda locked the front door of her cottage with a huge key, straightened her best hat – the one with the wax cherries and the stuffed bird – placed her black bag in the front basket of her rattly old bicycle and set off for town.

As she puffed up the steps to Miss Addle's Academy for Artistic Children, Grizelda could see, even from the outside, that a cleaner was badly needed.

The windows were grimy inside and out, and the paintwork around them more grey than white. Grizelda shook her head and tut-tutted at the discoloured brass doorknob and knocker on the big double front doors. She couldn't walk past without giving the letter-box a quick rub with her hanky.

Inside, however, she could see that some efforts had been made to make the school bright and cheerful. Home-made display boards (only *slightly* lopsided) lined the walls of the big airy entrance hall, and proudly displayed the colourful paintings and collages of the younger pupils. Shiny mobiles danced in the air, while papier-mâché sculptures and wooden carvings stood here and there. Near the foot of a broad staircase, a red-haired girl and a tall boy were moving another sculpture into place. They were laughing and chattering as they struggled with a lumpy, frog-like object, which reminded Grizelda of a bad dream she'd had once after a late supper of toasted cheese.

Grizelda coughed loudly, and the boy turned round. "Oh, sorry, we were so busy we didn't notice you there!

Er ... did you want to see Miss Addle? I'm afraid she's a bit ... um ... tied up just now." The children grinned at each other. "She's had to step in as a model for the seniors' drawing class, 'cos we can't afford to pay for a real artist's model this term, she says. My name's Ben and she's Sarah. Can we help?"

"Looks like *you're* the ones who could use some help around here," sniffed Grizelda, looking about her. "I don't know as I've ever seen so much dust in one place before."

"Yeah, that's what my mum says," agreed Sarah. "She says it's a disgrace and bad for my asthma, but my dad says it's not Miss Addle's fault that cleaners won't work for what she can pay them. He says my mum wouldn't work for it either."

"Does he, indeed!" said Grizelda thoughtfully, but before she could enquire further a tall, thin figure wrapped in trailing draperies appeared at the head of the stairs. It glided down the stairs, stretching out a hand towards Grizelda. For one moment Grizelda wondered whether the Academy had its own artistic ghost, but Sarah and Ben ran forward and as the "ghost" reached the bottom step they began to unwind it. What finally emerged was a pleasant, harassed-looking woman, dressed in an ordinary skirt and jumper.

"Thank you, children," she said, mopping her pink face with a piece of her discarded wrappings. "My, it was hot in there! I do wish the seniors had chosen something else for their drawing project! If I'd realized I had to be 'a mysterious veiled figure' this week I'd have worn a cotton frock today, or even my bathing suit!" She bundled up the material and handed it to Ben and Sarah. "Put these into the dressing-up box, please, on your way back to class. Isn't it almost time for your gym lesson? You'd better hurry, and don't forget to change your shoes!"

Sarah and Ben, arms full, hurried off. Miss Addle turned to Grizelda. "Good afternoon," she said warmly, still sounding rather flustered. "I am Miss Addle, the Headmistress of the Academy. Have you come to enroll a

new pupil, Mrs … er…?" Her eyes
brightened hopefully as she tugged at her
rumpled skirt and hastily smoothed her
faded, brown hair.

"The advertisement
said 'Cleaner wanted',"
said Grizelda firmly.
"It didn't say
anything about
pupils. If it was
pupils you wanted,
you should have
said so. My name is
Grizelda Grimthorpe,
and I've come about
the cleaning." And
not a moment too
soon, by the looks
of things, she
added to herself.

Miss Addle eyed Grizelda. A cleaner? Was she *quite* suitable? Really, with her short, dumpy figure, all that fly-away grey hair escaping from its untidy pony-tail and those bright green eyes, Mrs Grimthorpe looked – well, almost like a witch!

"I do need someone right away, Mrs Grimthorpe," she said doubtfully, "but I'm not sure … and really, you see, I can't pay much … so perhaps…"

As she spoke the phone rang in an office nearby. Miss Addle hurried in to answer it, leaving the door open behind her. While she waited for Miss Addle to return, Grizelda took a good look around. Once upon a time the Academy had been a grand house, with fine furniture and glittering chandeliers. Now the unswept halls and grimy stairways echoed to the running feet and happy voices of paint-smeared children, as a bell rang and classes surged from one room to another. Sunlight streamed in through a skylight window, and dust turned and danced in the shaft of golden light.

Through the open door of the Headmistress's office, Grizelda could see Miss Addle standing at her desk. She didn't seem to be enjoying her phone call. Her pink face had turned pale, and two little frown lines cut deep into her forehead. Suddenly she gasped and her quiet voice rose in protest. "Close the school? But, Mr Blockett, you can't do that!" A voice on the other end of the phone could be heard faintly, like a faraway duck quacking.

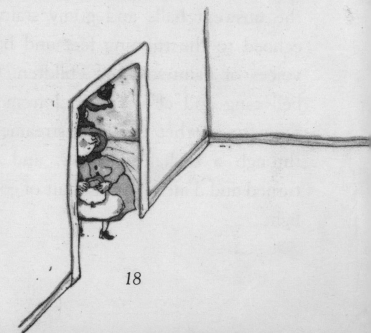

"Yes, I *know* it's a bit run-down at the moment, Mr Blockett, but we don't make much money and cleaners cost such a lot these days. But to say we should close the school ... the children *love* it here ... we can't just turn them away!"

"Quack! Quack!" went the phone for a long time while poor Miss Addle looked more and more unhappy.

Grizelda frowned. Suddenly, she decided that she liked the look of the school. It *was* dirty and messy, but that could be fixed. The school had a happy, friendly, lively atmosphere. Those two youngsters, Sarah and Ben, had actually looked pleased to see her. That was such a pleasant change from her lonely cottage. There, she had no one to talk to but her cat and that uppity crystal ball, and she had already spring-cleaned the cottage twice over until it shone. Close the school? Just when Grizelda had found herself the right job? No – not if *she* had anything to do with it!

Grizelda Grimthorpe fixed her bright green eyes on Miss Addle, twiddled her fingers – two bright purple sparks flew into the air – and muttered,

"Dirt and dust must now obey;
Grizelda Grimthorpe's come to stay!"

Miss Addle put down the phone, rubbed her forehead wearily and looked at Grizelda. "Yes, Mrs Grimthorpe, you'll do splendidly," she heard herself saying, though she felt sure she had really meant to say quite the opposite. "Can you start this afternoon? I'll show you where everything is kept – mops and brushes and so on."

"I'll use me own broom, if you don't mind," said Grizelda firmly. "It's used to me, like – it knows me ways. I don't want to go breaking in new brooms at my age."

Miss Addle blinked, hesitated for a moment, then she smiled. What difference could a broom make, after all?

"Do whatever you think is best, Mrs Grimthorpe," she said.

Chapter 2

Grizelda returned to the school later that day, just as the last few pupils straggled out through the big gates on their way home. Ben gave her a cheery smile and a thumbs-up sign as he passed.

A long, shiny, black car sat outside the front door. It looked important and official. Miss Addle came out of the school, nervous and flustered, with a man in a dark suit. He was frowning and shaking his head.

"If there isn't a big improvement, Miss Addle, I'm afraid we'll have no choice.

Can't have the pupils working in all this dust and dirt, can we? Parents are starting to complain! Doesn't look good! This building and the grounds would fetch a lot of money, you know. As trustees, we have to do our best…"

"But, Mr Blockett…" pleaded Miss Addle as he got into the back seat of the car.

He banged the door shut and wound down the window. "Remember, a big improvement, Miss Addle! I'll be keeping a close eye on things from now on!"

Grizelda watched the car sweep away, her green eyes hooded. Somebody's manners could do with a big improvement, she thought. Somebody needed to be taught a lesson! Grizelda set to work to do just that. She rolled up her sleeves, patted her broom and followed Miss Addle indoors.

Miss Addle looked pale and worn. "I think I'll go home and rest," she quavered. "It's been a very difficult day. Just do whatever you think is best, Mrs Grimthorpe. I'm afraid your job may not last for long, if Mr Blockett has his way. Oh, dear, if *only* we could prove that the school is worth saving!"

She gazed around the dusty hall, and absent-mindedly patted the nose of a lumpy black and white papier-mâché cow. "We used to win first prize in all the inter-schools art competitions, you know," she said. "Parents used to be proud to send their children here ... but somehow, all our materials have become so expensive. We don't charge high fees, you see, and it gets harder and harder to manage. Most of the parents couldn't pay higher fees even if we asked them to. Some of them can only just about manage as it is, and I won't ask them to pay more than they can afford."

With a last sad look around, Miss Addle went to fetch her coat, leaving Grizelda to her first evening's work.

Grizelda began cleaning the first classroom. Paper leaned against the walls in unsteady piles or stood in dusty rolls stacked in corners. Giant, economy-sized tins of glue dribbled stickily on to shelves and down to the floor. Tubes of paint, minus their tops, mingled their contents in sludgy brown puddles in the sink. In one corner stood a large clay-spattered bin, its lid half off. In another was a table, holding a cage labelled "Jeremiah". Something inside moved, and scuttered under a heap of wood shavings.

Grizelda looked closer. A long, pink, ribbed tail poked out of the shavings. She tickled it with a paintbrush. There was a small explosion among the shavings and a white rat appeared. A small, ordinary-looking rat with beady pink eyes. It sat up on its back legs and twitched its nose.

"Well," said Grizelda, "you're a sorry-looking specimen and no mistake!" The rat began washing its face, peering at her warily between swipes of its paws. "Hmm, 'spect you're as dusty as the rest of the place!"

Miss Addle's footsteps clicked past the classroom. She called goodbye. The front door shut with a bang which raised small clouds of dust and made the cage shake. The rat jumped nervously and disappeared under the wood shavings. Grizelda laughed and went back to work. She swept her broom – one of the old-fashioned, twiggy kind – through the dust, with a swishing sound which whispered through the empty classroom.

Chapter 3

Slowly, Grizelda Grimthorpe began to feel almost lonesome, all by herself in the echoing building. She wished there was someone to talk to while she worked. She glanced at the rat Jeremiah, which now peered from its cage with inquisitive eyes.

"Wish *you* could talk!" she said. She

gave it a long, considering look, then,
"Don't see why not," she said suddenly.
She twiddled her fingers – purple sparks
sizzled and spluttered like fireworks –
and muttered,

"By my bird and cherry hat,
What I need's a talking rat!"

The rat quivered, its outline shaking like something seen through a purple heat haze. Then it settled, solidified, and there sat a much larger white rat, sleek and fat, with purple eyes. It began to groom its silky coat from nose to tail, then, satisfied with its appearance, it made a low bow to Grizelda.

"Hmm," sniffed Grizelda, "handsome is as handsome does, my old mother used to say, but at least your manners are better than *some* as I could mention.

You'd better come out of there, for a start. I can't abide to see animals in cages."

"I quite agree, madam," said the rat in an unexpectedly sweet, high voice, "and I am indebted to you." As the cage door squeaked open he hopped out and surveyed the classroom, nose twitching, whiskers aquiver with excitement. "Such a lot to explore!"

"That's an idea, right enough," said Grizelda Grimthorpe. "I'll join you."

Clicking her fingers at the broom Grizelda muttered,

"Make the dust fly, besom broom,
Clean this higgledy-piggledy room!"

A swirl of lavender sparks settled over the broom where it stood propped against an easel. Jerkily, the broom rose and began to sweep briskly. "And mind you sweep *under* the desks too!" Grizelda reminded it firmly.

Behind her the lid fell off the clay-spattered bin. Jeremiah the rat balanced precariously on the edge of the bin, peering in. Inside, bundles wrapped in wet cloths gave off the strong, cold smell of damp clay. The rat sneezed.

"Clay!" said Grizelda happily. "I haven't made a good homunculus in a long time. I used to make 'em all the time when I was at school meself."

"Ah!" said the rat politely, "you were an artistic child, madam?"

Grizelda chuckled. "When I was a young apprentice witch, and *that's* many a year ago, making a few dozen little clay mannikins and bringing them to life was our usual punishment for being naughty – like writing a hundred lines would be nowadays."

"Ah!" said the rat, even more politely, "artistic and spirited, madam – artistic and spirited! A happy combination, I'm sure."

Grizelda watched the broom working away in the dusty corners. "What I need here," she murmured thoughtfully, "is a few extra pairs of hands, and I think I know where to get them."

She pulled out a heavy wodge of damp clay and thumped it down on a table. "*If I haven't forgotten how…*" she said, and unwrapped the bundle.

Chapter 4

Jeremiah watched with interest. Grizelda's fingers flew – pinching, prodding, tweaking the solid mass of clay. Purple, violet and lilac sparks sputtered and sizzled around her hands, hissing where they landed on the cold clay. The witch's lips moved silently, like someone reading an unseen story. Soon, the table held an array of stubby clay figures, each about twenty centimetres high, roughly fashioned but all individual. Their faces had round, hollow eyes (made by a pencil end) and blobby button noses. Grizelda stepped back, head on one side and lips pursed.

"Not my *best* effort," she said critically, "but it will have to do. Now, let's see ... how did the rest of the spell go..."

Jeremiah raised a paw. "How about –
'Little workers made of clay,
Never need a holiday'?"

"I can see you're going to come in
handy!" Grizelda said with a laugh,
repeating the rat's rhyme as she waved
her hands in an odd motion over the
collection of stumpy clay figures.

Jeremiah's eyes brightened. Each little
figure briefly gave off a bright purple
glow. As they changed colour their sticky
clay appearance changed too. There was
a sudden strong smell of lilac. (Jeremiah
sneezed again.) The dumpy figures

stirred, slowly turning their heads and stretching their fat little arms and legs, as if to check that they really worked. Chattering softly, they admired their own and each other's pink and purple colours. Then they all turned to Grizelda and waited, looking as expectant as their round faces allowed.

"Now then," said Grizelda briskly, "there's a lot to be done…"

As she marshalled her troops for The Great Clean-Up, no one noticed the faint crunch of gravel as a bicycle wobbled to a halt at the back door.

Mr Blockett climbed carefully off his bicycle and looked around. If anyone had been there to see him, they might have wondered at the change in his appearance. Gone was the smart dark suit and the polished shoes. In their place Mr Blockett wore ordinary jeans, an old sweatshirt and a pair of trainers. He no longer looked like a smart, respectable businessman. The only odd note was the clipboard he took out of his bicycle bag. Quietly he opened the back door and disappeared inside the school.

Meanwhile, Grizelda had organized the clay people – whom she called "claggies" – into a cleaning brigade. Swinging on curtains to shake out the dust, sliding down bannisters on toboggans made of dusters, venturing bravely under low cupboards in search of all the pencil ends, beads and fluff which make their homes in such spots, the claggies were an invincible army of dust-busters.

Grizelda's old broom, which jealously creaked and groaned in an alarming fashion when the claggies ventured too close, continued to swirl around the floor. Jeremiah joined in the spirit of the occasion and went from desk to desk, polishing off anything edible he could find – biscuit crumbs, furry old toffees and the like.

Grizelda floated herself up to the big chandelier in the hall, and became absorbed in washing and wiping every crystal dewdrop until it sparkled. She

hummed loudly
and a little off-key
as she dripped
water on to
anyone unwise
enough to linger
underneath.

Nobody noticed Mr Blockett. He
poked and pried in the kitchen, making
notes on his clipboard for the urgent
report he planned to make to the
Board of Trustees, recommending the
immediate closure and sale of the school.

He knew just who would like to buy such a valuable property, and there would be a fat reward in it for him if he could get old Milligrew, the Chairman, to agree that the school was too run-down and unsuccessful to continue.

Mr Blockett silently crept out of the old-fashioned kitchen, which to his disappointment had been kept clean and tidy. Time to look upstairs; he sneaked up the back stairs to the first floor. As he tiptoed along the corridor towards the main landing and the front staircase, he paused – what *was* that strange, droning sound, and those odd, soft, chattering noises?

Chapter 5

Mr Blockett proceeded cautiously. It would be embarrassing to have to explain his presence, if someone found him now. The crooning grew louder. He came to a turn in the corridor and peeped around the corner. To his astonishment, he saw a stout, grey-haired old woman slowly floating down through the air from a large sparkling crystal chandelier which hung over the stairwell just ahead of him! Water dripped from a cloth in one hand while her other hand steadied a floating yellow plastic bucket.

"I must be seeing things," moaned Mr Blockett. "It's all this overtime!" As though drawn by an irresistible force he crept out and looked over the bannister, down into the front entrance hall, where the strange old woman had just landed.

"Jeremiah!" she shouted.

From the nearest classroom a large white rat bustled out, wiping its mouth. It bowed politely and said in clear, fluting tones, "You called, madam?"

Mr Blockett raised a trembling hand to his forehead and sank to his knees. He closed his eyes and began to count to ten silently. Four… Five… All a dream!

... Six... Seven... Just overwork! ...
Eight... Nine ... something cold brushed
against his hand. He opened his eyes and
found himself staring into two round,
hollow eyes in a fat little purple face.

Mr Blockett let out a strangled yell –
which seriously alarmed the poor claggy
– fell straight over backwards with a
crash, got to his feet and ran!

Darkness had fallen before Grizelda
Grimthorpe felt satisfied with the
changed appearance of Miss Addle's
Academy. Floors gleamed; shelves were
models of ordered neatness, with papers,
paints and other bits and pieces all stored
away in labelled containers.

Finally the claggies assembled, chattering and squeaking softly, back by the clay bin (now minus its splatters of old, dried clay). Jeremiah, who had grown quite attached to them all, looked anxiously at Grizelda.

"What now, madam?" he asked quietly.

"Time to undo my spells," said Grizelda.

"Everything, madam?" said Jeremiah sadly. He had so enjoyed his new powers and appearance.

Grizelda hesitated. "I must turn the claggies back to clay," she said slowly. "They won't last past midnight anyway, and if I leave them, it'll only spoil the clay they're made of, letting it dry out. That was a powerful spell I put on it, and it may leave some magic in the clay, but that won't do any harm. No one will notice. Waste not, want not! But you, now ... that's another matter."

Jeremiah looked hopeful.

With sudden decision, Grizelda declared, "I know! If no one but me can see the changes in you, or hear you speak, then what they don't know won't hurt 'em, will it? And I have a feeling you're going to come in very handy here! I'll need someone who can keep an eye on things for me during the day, and give me a bit of a hand – I mean, a bit of a paw – at night."

With a twiddle of fingers and a shower of sparks, Grizelda muttered,
"Back to clay let claggies go,
But Jeremiah none shall know.
By my bird and cherry hat,
None shall hear a talking rat!"

Where the claggies had stood, there was now a heap of clay, to which a faint smell of lilac still clung. Ignoring Jeremiah's wistful sigh, Grizelda Grimthorpe gathered it up briskly and stuffed it back into the clay bin, fastening the lid down firmly.

"Time I was off home," she said,
putting on her coat and hat. A final
glance around, a satisfied nod, and she
picked up her broom and was gone.

Jeremiah watched from the darkened classroom as her plump figure on the old broom sailed across the high school gates and over the trees on the horizon. The silvery face of the moon shone down on the big white rat as it turned away from the window and pattered across the empty classroom. For a moment the rat paused by the clay bin, patted it gently and sighed. What a Friday this had been – the strangest Friday ever, perhaps.

Chapter 6

When Monday morning arrived, Miss Addle could scarcely believe her eyes! The Academy looked like a different school altogether. The teachers and children were all astonished by the change. In the new, improved, *ordered* Academy everyone worked harder.

From then on, every day, just as the

children were leaving, Grizelda arrived to clean up that day's spilled paint, and to sweep and dust every corner. Jeremiah was equally particular about eating up every dropped crumb or apple core! Ben and Sarah would wait at the front steps for Grizelda's arrival, to show her their latest art work or a new game they'd just learnt. Soon Grizelda would be surrounded by laughing pupils, all talking at once and clamouring for her attention.

That summer, Miss Addle entered the school in the annual county art exhibition for schools. To everyone's surprise – everyone except one old, green-eyed lady and one white rat, that is – the entries from Miss Addle's Academy for Artistic Children took First Prize in all categories, with a Special Distinction being awarded by the judges for the clay sculptures.

"Inspired effort ... almost magical ... enchanting vision..." were just some of the comments. "The clay almost seems to have a life of its own..." said one judge, who came closer than he could ever have known to the truth.

Miss Addle was delighted to receive a visit of congratulations from old Sir James Milligrew, the Chairman of the Academy Board of Trustees. He waved an important-looking envelope in the air.

"Good news, Miss Addle! Good news!" he cried. "The Board of Trustees asked the local authority for some help in funding the Academy, and your pupils have just done so well in the county art competition that they have agreed! Our money worries are over!"

"Pity about young Blockett," he said as he was leaving. "Between you and me, Miss Addle, he went a bit peculiar – had to go away for a long rest, you know.

Wrote the most extraordinary report on the school – sheer gibberish about talking rats, and old ladies flying about with yellow buckets. Saw little purple men, you know – overwork, poor fellow!"

Miss Addle stood at the foot of the front steps, watching Sir James' shiny black car drive away. A short, stout figure on a rattly old bicycle pedalled slowly up the drive.

Really, thought Miss Addle, if I didn't know better, I'd swear Mrs Grimthorpe was a witch!

The End